DEAR LEVI

LETTERS FROM THE OVERLAND TRAIL

ELVIRA WOODRUFF

illustrated by BETH PECK

SCHOLASTIC INC.
New York   Toronto   London   Auckland   Sydney
Mexico City   New Delhi   Hong Kong

ISBN 0-439-05605-5

Text copyright © 1994 by Elvira Woodruff.
Illustrations copyright © 1994 by Beth Peck.
Map copyright © 1994 by Anita Karl and James Kemp.
Cover art copyright © 1998 by Bill Maughan.
All rights reserved.
Published by Scholastic Inc., 555 Broadway, New York, NY 10012,
by arrangement with Alfred A. Knopf, Inc.
SCHOLASTIC and associated logos are trademarks and/or registered
trademarks of Scholastic Inc.

24 23 22 21 20 19 18 17 16 15 14   6 7 8 9/0

Printed in the U.S.A.   40

First Scholastic printing, November 1998

Acknowledgments

For all the "gems" I've met on my travels across the country. With special thanks for inspiring teachers such as Ms. Ina Esteva of Sweetwater Elementary in Miami, Florida, and Mrs. Sue Williams of Five Points Elementary in Bangor, Pennsylvania. For the many fine librarians such as Joan Welsh of Indian Hill Elementary of Cincinnati, Ohio, and Carolyn Malhoit of Scottsdale, Arizona. For the outstanding reading specialists like Norma Bossard of Miami, Florida. And of course what keeps me smiling as I trek from state to state are the great kids who can be found in each and every school. For your many warm welcomes and smiling faces, I thank you all!

—E. W.

Preface

When Levi Ives died at the age of seventy-one in 1913, he was a wealthy man. To his wife, Hanna, and his daughter, Ella, he left great property holdings, investments, and money. But it was to his unborn grandchild that he left his most prized possessions. As he stated in his will:

> In the event that children are born to my daughter, Ella, her firstborn shall have the letters and the button book, which have meant more to me than all the possessions I have acquired in this life. It would please me to know that they were given to Ella's first child on the eve of his or her ninth birthday.

Several years later Ella Ives Brently gave birth to a son. She named him Austin and on the eve of his ninth birthday gave him a packet of letters and a large book covered in worn scarlet velvet.

OREGON
TERRITORY
Site of Ives claim

Columbia R.

BLUE MTS.

Ft. Boise

Snake R.

NEBRASKA
TERRITORY
(1854)

Devil's
Gate

Independence
Rock

Soda
Springs
(Steamboat
Springs)

Elkhorn R.

Ft. Laramie

Platte R.

UTAH
TERRITORY

KANSAS TERRIT

(1854

CALIF.

NEW MEXICO
TERRITORY

INDI

Pacific
Ocean

TEXAS

The Overland
Trail, 1851

MEXICO

CANADA

N

OTA
ORY

WIS.

MICH.

IOWA

ILL.

IND.

OHIO

Sudbury

PA.

N.Y.

VT.

N.H.

MASS.

R.I.
CONN.

N.J.

MD.

DEL.

MO.

KY.

VA.

ARK.

TENN.

N.C.

S.C.

MISS.

ALA.

GA.

LA.

FLA.

Atlantic
Ocean

Gulf of Mexico

0   Miles   300

© 1994 A. Karl / J. Kemp

Dear Levi,

I am writing to you from the state of Ohio, and even though it is only a week's drive from home in Sudbury, I feel as if I'm already a long way from Pennsylvania. I wonder what I will feel like after traveling almost three thousand miles to Oregon? Tired, I reckon, after all that walking!

None of the men or older boys ride in the wagons, as that would be cowardly, seeing how the oxen have such heavy loads to pull. Many of the women and children walk also. Some of the younger boys do nothing but hunt for firewood and frogs (the frogs being for their own amusement), but since I am twelve years old, I work right alongside the men most of the time.

My day starts at about four thirty in the morning when I have to cut out the oxen from the herd and drive them to the wagon for yoking and hitching. Then I help Mr. Morrison check over the running gear. We have breakfast and are ready to travel by seven o'clock. We're on the road till noon. Then we unhitch the oxen and set the stock to graze before taking our lunch. After

an hour or so we hitch up again and go on for another four or five hours. I can tell you that walking fifteen to twenty miles a day can tire the strongest legs. I have much to write you about, but the fire is getting low and I need to rest up for tomorrow's drive.

Your brother, Austin

Dear Levi,

We now have twenty-four wagons in our train, as two new parties joined us yesterday. Everyone is in good spirits, and there is much talk among the men about the gold mines at Sutter's Mill in California, though most of the families in this party have Oregon fever and are looking to settle along the shores of the Columbia River.

I surely hated leaving you behind in Pennsylvania, but you know I couldn't pass up the opportunity to go out to Oregon and see about Pa's claim. He staked everything he owned in this world on a new start for us. In his last letter he told Miss Amelia that should any accident befall him we should seek out Mr. Ezra Zikes, for he had promised Pa to look after his affairs and protect his claim for us.

Now that Pa is gone I am hoping that Mr. Zikes will help me to get work and lodging at the lumber camp where Pa worked. Once you're old enough, Levi, you can come, too. Till then, mind Miss Amelia and don't go chasing after her chickens too much.

I am glad that Miss Amelia secured me passage with her cousin's family. The Morrisons have a fine wagon, and I reckon they're glad to have me with them, as they only have three little girls of their own. Mr. Morrison said yesterday that he never saw a twelve-year-old boy who could "ride in oxen" the way I do. I wish Pa were alive so he could see me. Tell Miss Amelia that Mrs. Morrison is almost as good a cook as she is. We had baked suckeyes, stewed apples, cooked meat with beans, and coffee for breakfast this morning.

We met a family in the wagon behind us, name of Hickman, and they have a boy called Frank who is just my age. He has some fine marbles and a snakeskin in good condition. When we talked about breakfast, he said they call suckeyes "pancakes" where he comes from. Don't that sound strange? There is also a boy in the wagon ahead by the name of Hiram Buckner. He is a short boy full of tall tales. Yesterday he told me that he had once caught a catfish that weighed a hundred pounds. (Which must have been tricky since Hiram can't weigh more than seventy-five pounds himself, soaked and wet.)

Frank, on the other hand, seems like a quiet sort of

fellow, and it took a lot of prying to get him to talk at all. His father is a big, meanspirited man who is always hollering and spitting juice. I'm glad Mr. Morrison is not that way.

My job is to keep the cattle fed and watered and to help with the driving. I also milk the cows, hunt and fish, and help with finding firewood. We hope to reach the Columbia River in four months' time. Although I don't expect to be able to send you letters very often, I'll write them anyway and mail them when I can.

Each night before I turn in I have to check on the cattle and horses, and sometimes when it's pitch-black all around, with only the sounds of the night critters and the wind, I get to feeling lonesome and I begin to wonder about so much. I wonder about the Indians and the buffalo and the river crossings.

I worry about the river even more than the Indians, because in a short time we expect to cross Miller's Creek. I have not had the courage to tell Mr. Morrison that I have never learned to swim, and it weighs on my mind something awful.

I best close now and rest up for tomorrow's drive. Don't forget your big brother, who thinks of you often.

Dear Levi,

I hope this letter finds you fit and dry. We've gone clear across Ohio and through Indiana. It's been raining on and off for the last three days, and we had to make camp without a fire. It rained so hard last night that the water soaked right through the wagon cover and Mrs. Morrison and the girls came down to sleep under the wagon with me. They made such a racket, it reminded me of Miss Amelia's henhouse at feeding time!

Charlotte, the oldest, is three years younger than you, and she's the bossiest six-year-old you'd ever want to meet. She's always demanding that I pick her up and give her a swing-around, like I used to do with you. Lucy, the two-year-old, has a head of red corkscrew curls, and she's forever getting into mischief. Then there's the baby, Mattie, who's got a perfectly round bald head and smiles at the slightest nudge.

This morning after breakfast I was leaning against the side of the wagon, taking a stone out of my shoe, when I saw Charlotte and Lucy fixing up a breakfast of mud pies. Lucy, feeling generous, offered one to the baby, who almost ate it, but decided to squeeze it and then throw it instead. Lucy and Charlotte joined in, and before long all three were squealing as the mud went flying.

With so much rain, we've been getting stuck in one blame mudhole after another. I sure miss a warm bed and dry clothes. You know how I hate to get wet. Of course, this is nothing compared with Miller's Creek. Now, that was wet! I finally owned up to Mr. Morrison, just before we got there, that I was not a swimmer. And although he seemed disappointed, for he needs my help with getting the wagon and the cattle across the water, he was not angry.

"Austin," he says, "a boy's got to know how to swim if he's going to be journeying out to the territories." So with each creek and branch we've had to cross, I've been getting swimming lessons! Mr. Morrison is very patient, and for the first few lessons we stayed in the shallow parts. I don't mind as much when the water is clear and I can see the bottom. I still cross deep water with a rope tied around me, especially if the current's swift, but I've lost some of my fear (had to, since there is more darn water in this country than you can imagine). When we crossed a branch last week we almost lost a horse, and Mr. Morrison and I had to go after him to keep him from heading downstream! Mr. Morrison said when the water warms up, he's going to teach me the backstroke.

Hiram Buckner, Frank Hickman, and I went out hunting the other day, and Frank and I each got a rabbit. Hiram didn't get anything. He said his aim was off on account of his having hunted so much big game.

"And what big game would that be?" Frank wanted to know.

"Buffalo," Hiram replies without a blink. Now, seeing how Hiram has lived in Pennsylvania all his life, I had to wonder just how he could find any buffalo there. Hiram got a funny look on his face when we mentioned this, and he started pulling on his ear. "Oh, they're around," he says. "Not many, but every once in a while we'd get a few." Frank and I couldn't help but grin at this, though that didn't stop Hiram. He went on to tell us a long tale about how he and his pa had brought down a buffalo out in their cornfield back of their house with only one shot! I never met anyone who could tell such barefaced lies with such an honest-looking face.

I've got a bad case of poison ivy on my legs, but I

picked some jewelweed to rub over it, so I'm hoping it clears up soon. Levi, I'm saving stones and bird feathers for your collections, like I promised. Found some fine blue bird feathers and a round speckled stone that looks just like the egg of a guinea hen.

Your brother, Austin

Dear Levi,

We camped last night three miles east of Chariton Point. This prairie is nothing but flat, flat, flat! It's a strange sight to be looking out before you and not be able to see one single tree. Without them or hills or houses the sky seems much bigger, and it's almost as if you're closer to it somehow.

Charlotte and Lucy have come down with the mumps and Mrs. Morrison is much relieved, for she feared it was the cholera. We passed thirteen graves yesterday along the trail. One was marked JOHN FRIPPS, 14 YEARS, DIED OF THE FEVER. Mrs. Morrison and the other women brewed up a big pot of preventive, throwing in all kinds of herbs and roots. All us children had to drink some down. Frank drank his down in one gulp, but Hiram and I kept taking little sips of ours, and it was so awful tasting that we finally spit out the rest behind some bushes. Hiram's mouthful landed on a beetle, which we kept a close eye on to see what effect the medicine would have. That little critter scratched a hole in the dirt and buried himself down into it real quick.

Sometimes the days fly by, and other times they crawl along as if they were stuck in molasses. We had to stop twice last week to fix broken wheels and have not made many miles. Frank, who is usually good company, had been feeling poorly, on account of a bad toothache. He didn't want to tell his ma about it, 'cause he was afraid it would have to be pulled. But it was hurting so bad the other day that Frank couldn't keep from moaning out loud. Sure enough, his ma took a look and told me and Hiram to fetch Mr. Belshaw.

Poor Frank's face went all white when he heard this, for Mr. Belshaw, being a smith, is also a tooth-puller. He's a powerful big man with a great shiny bald head and lots of black hair coming out of his nose. Hiram and I went to fetch him, and I swear my jaw started to ache just looking at the man! When we told him about Frank, Mr. Belshaw scratched his fat stomach and went up into his wagon, coming out presently with a heavy pair of pincers. "Poor Frank," Hiram whispered. "Too bad he drank up all his preventive. Would have been better to die of the fever than face those things." I shuddered at the sight of the big black pincers in Mr. Belshaw's hand.

When we got to the Hickmans' wagon, we found Frank sitting on a stump, with his pa and some other men standing by. Hiram was so overcome with emotion that he pressed his prize possession, his fossil stone, into Frank's hand and told him he could keep it for luck. But Hiram's generosity was lost on Frank, who couldn't take his eyes off those big black pincers. As Mr. Hickman and another man held Frank down, Mr. Belshaw dabbed a rag soaked in whiskey into Frank's mouth and then went on to explain that the tooth could come out one of two ways—easy or hard. If it went easy, it could be twisted right out, but if it went hard and broke beneath the gum, Mr. Belshaw said he would have to use his knife to cut the gum on each side of the root and dig it out piece by piece. On hearing this I thought Frank was about to faint with fear.

"It don't hurt no more, really it don't," he began to whimper. But this didn't satisfy Mr. Belshaw, who I suppose hears much the same from most of his patients after such a speech.

Hiram and I were beginning to feel poorly ourselves and didn't think we could stomach watching the operation, especially if it went hard. But seeing how Frank was our good friend, we thought we should at least listen, so we stationed ourselves on the other side of the wagon, where we could hear everything.

I'm glad to report that it went easy, with only a lot of little whimpering and one long holler coming out of Frank when the tooth come out. Afterward Hiram and I went to have a look at the rotten tooth. It didn't seem all that rotten to me, although some smaller boys offered to trade Frank some marbles for it. He said he wanted to hold on to it for a while. Seeing how Frank looked so recovered, Hiram asked for his fossil back, but Frank would not give it up.

I wish you could hear him whistle now.

Your brother, Austin

Dear Levi,

This prairie seems to stretch on forever. Mr. Morrison took sick with dysentery yesterday, so I had to do much of the driving today. The oxen gave me little trouble, except for the biggest, Big Abe, who tended to have ideas of his own on which direction the wagon should take.

At supper Mrs. Morrison sat beside me in her rocking chair. It's a strange sight to see her in the chair, as no one else thought to bring such a big piece of furniture. But Mrs. Morrison said she would not leave Pennsylvania without it, since it is her prize possession, and so she left behind a whole trunk of good linen, for there was no room in the wagon for both. At each campsite she hauls the rocker out of the wagon, and when her cooking is done she'll sit and sew or tend to Mattie, who wants her lap. As I watched Mrs. Morrison rocking and stroking Mattie's hair, I felt shivers run down my back. It called up a memory of Ma, a memory of us together in a rocking chair doing that very same thing when I was little. I was so surprised, for it was something that I hadn't thought of in a long, long time. I know you can't remember Ma, as she died when you were just born, but to me Mrs. Morrison seems very much like her, with her honey-colored hair and her gentle ways. I am glad to be traveling with the Morrisons.

Your brother, Austin

Dear Levi,

We have made only ten miles since last I wrote. Had to spend a good part of yesterday waiting for the Hickmans' broken axle to be repaired. I have met an amazing man. His name is Reuben McAlister Rice. Everyone calls him Reuben. He works for the head man, Mr. Hart. Reuben's job is to cook for Mr. Hart and the men who work for him. Reuben has crisscrossed the country back and forth to the territories for the last ten years, and before that he went across the ocean to Europe. I have never met anyone like him. He has a big red beard and bushy red eyebrows to match. In his ear he wears a little gold earring, and on his boots are Mexican spurs made of silver. But the two best things about Reuben are his coat and his stories.

First I'll tell you about his stories. No one can tell a story like Reuben, not even Hiram, 'cause Reuben can make his voice sound like a little bitty baby one minute and an old crackling crow the next. He can grunt and groan like any critter you ever heard, and he knows more bird calls than old Calvin Heppel.

21

Last night Hiram, Frank, and I were lying on our backs looking up at the sky. The clouds had finally cleared out, and there was a blaze of shooting stars. We had a good time trying to guess where the next star would fall. Then Reuben came over and told us a good story about a man who had a shooting star land on his barn and how all the animals began to talk after that. First he would use their animal voice, and then he would have them talking as people would. We laughed and laughed to hear the chickens complaining like a bunch of old biddies.

Now about Reuben's coat. He always wears this great sheepskin coat that's got buttons sewn all over it, up the arms and across the front and back. Frank wondered if Reuben had ever been in the circus, on account of having such a festive coat.

Reuben shook his head and smiled. "This old coat comes from the circus, all right. The circus of life." He went on to tell us that he had been collecting buttons for years, as he traveled all over the world. He had all kinds, colors, and shapes, from silver and pewter to wood and cloth covered, and each one had a history. There was a shiny brass button from George Washington's uniform and a ruby-inlaid button from the king of Spain's breeches. Reuben even had a bone button, made of human bone, taken off a pirate's coat. We all wanted to touch that one! It's hard to know with Reuben if he's telling a tale or the truth, but that bone button sure made me nervous when I touched it.

Reuben told us that he travels with a big button book. "I never heard of such a book," says Hiram. So Reuben went on to explain that he bought it off a tailor who had once made a cape for the king of England. On each page of the book are velvet envelopes, and each envelope is filled with buttons. Reuben says he won't travel anywhere without his button book. When he meets up with a new friend, he offers to trade a button from his book. With each trade he sews the new button onto his coat, and that way he has something to remember the person by, and his coat keeps changing with every new button he adds.

I think of you often, Levi, and I'm hoping it won't be too long before we can be together again.

Your brother, Austin

Dear Levi,

Crossed the Elkhorn River today. Before we did, we discovered that one of our oxen was missing. Frank, Hiram, and I spent a good three hours hunting him down. Finally found him in some brush about two miles away. As we rounded him up and led him back, we saw a line of wagons, some three hundred or more, stretching out as far as a body could see. Everyone was waiting to cross the river. There is no ferry here, and Mr. Morrison and the other men were busy making one out of a wagon bed. Everything had to be hauled out of the wagons, and then each wagon was taken apart. A strong rope was stretched across the river with a wagon bed attached to it in the middle. Mr. Belshaw and some other men had swum across the river and were waiting at one end of the rope. Everything had to be got across a little at a time. I was busy with the cattle, and Mrs. Morrison was busy emptying out the wagon. No one took notice that Lucy had wandered off.

Then suddenly as Frank, Hiram, and I were standing on the shore, we heard Mrs. Morrison calling out for her. Charlotte came running up to me, crying that Lucy was gone and no one could find her. I was about to turn around to search in the woods, when I caught sight of something white in the water upstream. It was Lucy! The water was up to her knees, and she was walking farther and farther into it, as calm as you please.

I gave a shout to her, and then I took off with Hiram and Frank following behind me. We all rushed into the water and got to her just as she stumbled and was about to be carried away by the current. When we carried her back, everybody was hollering and cheering as if we were three heroes. Truth is, it all happened so fast, I didn't have time to give it much thought. I don't know who Mrs. Morrison kissed more—me or Lucy!

But the best part of it was that Reuben come up to us and says, "I reckon I'd be proud to have three friends the likes of you. You can stop by my wagon first thing tomorrow, if you've a mind to trade some buttons."

It took us till sundown to get the wagons and cattle across the river. It was a long day, and everyone was glad to be on the other side. All I can think about to-night is going into Reuben's wagon and looking through the big old button book.

Your brother, Austin

Dear Levi,

Stepping into the wagon of Reuben McAlister Rice was more of an adventure than I had reckoned on. The first thing I noticed was a big old tabby cat sitting on a barrel. It was staring at me with the greenest eyes you ever saw. The cat had a strange way about it, though, as it sat perfectly still, almost as if it were looking straight through me. But the wagon was so crammed full of sights I soon left off looking at the cat and turned to see Reuben's great coat hanging from a hook.

And just above that was a rope strung with bones. (I hope they were animal bones, but I don't know for sure.) There were dried flowers, bunches of weeds, and long, gnarly roots hanging everywhere. Reuben told us that he had spent some time traveling with a "root doctor," who taught him all he knew about the art of healing.

"You can cure any sickness with the right root, herb, or concoction," Reuben was quick to tell us on opening a big wooden box. We looked inside to see a collection of little green glass jars he keeps all lined up in rows.

He calls them his healing jars. Reuben went on to pull out a jar filled with sparrow feathers and another filled with skunk grease. Reuben claims that skunk grease rubbed on "the afflicted area" cures the rheumatism. He's also got a little bottle of red worm oil that he says will do the same. Frank, Hiram, and I all agreed that if we had to, we'd rub down with worm oil any day rather than with the grease from some old skunk.

Reuben laughed and said he thought we wouldn't be needing to worry about rheumatism till we were a mite older. I was standing by his coat and I couldn't help myself—I just had to run my fingers over some of those wonderful buttons. He caught sight of me and nodded.

Reuben stared at the coat for a long spell and then he said, "This big world is peopled with an amazing assortment of characters. You can just see for yourself how each of those buttons stands out so unique. And it's the same with people. They're like so many different gemstones, precious and shining in different ways and colors. Now, I want you lads to take your time and concentrate." Then he reached into a trunk and pulled out a big velvet-covered book.

Suddenly Reuben's voice got low and whispery, and I felt goose bumps on the back of my neck.

"Each of you can choose one button," he whispered. "But take your time and choose carefully. Pick only the one that calls out to you."

As his hands opened the book, it was as if he were opening a pirate's chest of jewels. Sewn onto each page were two velvet envelopes filled with buttons. And the funny thing is I would never have thought to give a button so much importance, it being more women's work, what with sewing and the like. But Levi, I swear we all were speechless, Frank, Hiram, and me, as Reuben emptied one envelope and then another, page after page. I never knew there could be such a collection of buttons.

Hiram didn't take but five minutes before he reached for a long bone button. "Elk, not human," Reuben assured us. Then Frank found a button made of copper. Reuben rubbed it on his shirt sleeve and it shined up real pretty.

I took the longest time choosing. There were so many envelopes in that big book. And each handful of buttons that he pulled out looked better than the last. But I kept waiting for one to "call out to me" the way Reuben said it should. Besides, I knew I was choosing for you, and I wanted to pick the best.

Hiram was yanking on my sleeve and I knew I had to decide soon, when all of a sudden Reuben opened an envelope and pulled out two perfectly round buttons. They looked like pearl with swirls of blue and pink in them. Reuben said they were "abalone shell." The best part was one of them had swirls in the shape of a face. It reminded me of the face of the moon. Then I remembered how Pa used to tell us stories of the old man in the moon, and how you'd always pester him to tell you another. So this moon-faced button was calling out to me and I knew it was the perfect one for you.

We had each cut off the buttons on our jackets, and when we handed them to Reuben in exchange, I looked down at my own plain wooden button and imagined what it would look like sewn onto such a coat. I wished that I had one that sparkled or stood out in some way. It seemed very ordinary indeed. It was as if Reuben had read my mind, for he held my button up and said straight away, "A fine button here. It is of a good hardwood, strong and lasting, walnut, I think."

He smiled, and I smiled back, and as we turned to leave I took another look at the big tabby. He was staring same as before.

"He don't move much, does he?" I said. Reuben gave out a little snort and scratched his whiskers.

"Old Bill there hasn't moved for the last two years."

"But how does he do it?" Frank wanted to know. "I never knowed a cat to sit still for two whole years."

"Unless he got some hex on him," Hiram added, squinting into Old Bill's steady green eyes. Suddenly we heard Frank's pa stomping around outside and calling for Frank to come and finish his chores. We took a peek outside of the wagon and saw that he was carrying a hickory switch. He looked so mean, Hiram and I were afraid he might take the switch to us just for being Frank's friends. But he didn't.

In the afternoon I asked Mrs. Morrison to sew your moon button on my coat, where I'll keep it till next we meet.

It was a very great morning, we all agreed later that night as we sat around the fire. Only Hiram thought it could have been better.

"How?" Frank wanted to know. And you know what Hiram answers?

"We should have unscrewed that jar of skunk grease. It would have been good fun to take a whiff." Only Hiram could imagine that snorting skunk grease would be fun!

Your brother, Austin

Dear Levi,

I've taken sick today with a sour stomach. The girls were down with it yesterday and were up and running this morning, so I suppose I shall recover. Last night Mr. Morrison and I went over his maps. He is teaching me to read them. Besides his map of the trail, he also has maps of many different countries like England, Spain, and France. Mr. Morrison loves maps because, he says, "They give a man room to wander, if only in his imagination."

He also said, "We can travel anywhere together," and with his finger guiding mine, we made our way around the world. He knows all the countries and their mountain ranges by heart, and named them for me. He laughed when I stopped in the middle of the Atlantic Ocean to look for a sunken pirate ship. He said that many pirates buried their treasure along the coast of Spain, so that's where we went looking for some. I could have stayed up all night with him, laughing and wandering around the world, looking for buried treasure.

Your brother, Austin

Dear Levi,

Mr. Morrison says we're two hundred miles or so from Fort Laramie, and if we keep on as we are, we should be there by the beginning of next month. I wish I could hear from you somehow, Levi. I think about you and hope you're well. Frank's little brother Abraham often tags along with us, and sometimes Frank gets so mad. He says he hates to have him always "nosing around." It makes me a little homesick, thinking about how mad I used to get at you for doing the same thing!

After supper, as the men were sitting around the fire, word came down from the wagons ahead that Indians had been sighted some ten miles away. No one seems to know if they're friendly or not. Mr. Hickman let out a hoot as soon as he heard about them. He bragged that he wasn't going to end his trip without "shootin' me an Injun," and a few of the other men laughed at this.

Mr. Morrison did not laugh. He said that Mr. Hickman had no right to kill anyone, Indian or no. Mr. Hickman did not like the sound of that. His eyes got all bulgy, and the big veins along his neck looked as if they were going to pop. He spit some juice not far from Mr. Morrison's boot and then said, "I don't suppose a coward would know much about killing Injuns."

Everyone got real quiet, and I was afraid for Mr. Morrison, as he is a thin man and not as big as Mr. Hickman. Finally Mr. Yardly, an older man, said that he thought we best be getting to bed, so as to be ready tomorrow for whatever the day might bring. Then he got up and walked right over to Mr. Morrison.

"I sure would appreciate it if you'd give me a hand with that splintered wheel tomorrow, Tom," he says. "You know the one I was telling you about. Come on, I'll show which one I mean." Mr. Morrison stood up slowly and looked Mr. Hickman right in the eye. I was holding my breath, wondering what would happen next. But Mr. Hickman looked away, and everyone else started talking again.

Frank's face went all red as he sat beside me, twisting his snakeskin around a twig. He was so embarrassed by his pa's remarks that he lowered his eyes and wouldn't look at anyone. All of a sudden it felt strange to be sitting next to him, and I couldn't think of anything to say. Hiram offered to tell us about the Indians that had attacked their house last spring and how he had fought them off single-handed, but neither of us wanted to hear about it.

I can't help feeling uneasy about all this, and wonder what will come tomorrow.

Your brother, Austin

Dear Levi,

We traveled twelve miles today and there was no sign of Indians. I think I ate more sand than biscuit for breakfast. The wind blew up clouds of dust and sand so thick a body could get lost in them. By afternoon the winds were so high that the women couldn't even make a fire to cook on. We are still in Nebraska Territory, camped on the bank of Loup Fork along the Platte River. We are waiting for our turn to cross. It is very dangerous, as parts of the riverbed are made of quicksand. There is a ferry, and for three dollars they will tow the wagon. Mr. Morrison and I will have to swim the stock, though. I've been getting better at this, as Mr. Morrison gives me lessons whenever he's able and there's water about.

Mr. Morrison spends a good deal of his free time teaching me things and talking to me about farming. He even calls me "son" now and again. I know lots of folks call boys that, but I like hearing it just the same.

Frank says that when we get farther along in the territories, he's aiming to run away. His pa took a hickory switch to him for being late with his chores and then again for spilling a bucket of water. His mother, although never mean to Frank, is stony-faced and never smiles. I told Frank that he's welcome to come live with you and me once we get settled. I don't know how such a nice fellow could have such a mean pa. When Frank tripped and dropped the bucket, he cut his foot on a rock. It pained him to walk with the cut, but that didn't make any difference to Mr. Hickman, who insisted he keep to his work.

After supper Hiram, Frank, and I went looking for some cobwebs to lay over Frank's cut. Hiram says that cobwebs are the best cure for a wound. At first Frank wasn't so sure he wanted cobwebs laid on him, but then Hiram called him a coward and said he'd used cobwebs lots of times to cure his cuts. Hiram went on to say that he didn't think there was much of anything that could scare him, not pirates, or lightning, or even rotting dead bodies.

We were poking through some brush, searching for cobwebs, with Hiram still going on about all he wasn't a-scared of, when we came upon a den of prairie dogs. They gave out some yelps, but that was nothing com-

Dear Levi,

I wish I never lived to see what I had to see today. And there's no telling what will come because of it tomorrow. It all started last night with a terrible storm. The wind in this territory can be very fierce, so fierce it pulled off the Yardlys' wagon cover, and the rain was coming down so hard that everything was soaked through within an hour.

When morning finally came, two oxen were found killed by lightning, and most of the cattle had scattered. Hiram, Frank, and I spent a long time searching for them and herding them back to camp. The going was awfully slow, as it rained on and off and we were in mud up to our hubs. Everyone was worn out from being awake most of the night and feeling cold and soaked through. I was walking with Frank beside his wagon when word suddenly came down that there were Indians up ahead.

On hearing this, Mr. Hickman climbed up into his wagon and came back down with his rifle.

"They didn't say whether they were friendly or not," I whispered to Frank.

"Don't make no difference to my pa," Frank said. "He's been wanting to kill himself an Injun ever since we started this trip."

I wondered what these Indians would be like and if they would put up a good fight against Mr. Hickman and his rifle. I supposed they would have only their bows and arrows, though maybe they'd have poison arrows and tomahawks, too.

We quickened our pace, as everyone was anxious to set eyes on the Indians. When they finally arrived, they were in small groups. They did not look as if they wanted to fight, for there were women among them, and the men were not aiming their arrows. They were offering berries, beads, and moccasins for trade. Some of their women traded berries for bread, and Mr. Taylor traded a lot of hard crackers for a pair of moccasins from a tall, proud-looking Indian man. But after we had started on, the Indian came running back up to Mr. Taylor's wagon, making a fuss and pointing to the moccasins he had traded. Mr. Taylor would not give them back, as the Indian had already eaten some of the crackers. It was clear the Indian did not understand that the crackers were all Mr. Taylor was willing to give for the moccasins.

I was glad to see Reuben slow his wagon to a stop and proceed to get down. I knew he would try and sort things out between the two, but before Reuben could reach their wagon, Mr. Hickman had come around with his rifle. He yelled for the Indian to be off, but the Indian wouldn't budge, except to reach out to take the moccasins back. That's when Mr. Hickman took aim and was about to shoot—just as one of the Indian women stepped into the fray. She was trying to give back the bread when the shot rang out. I saw her drop down into the grass beside the wagon as the smell of gunshot filled my nostrils.

The other Indians all scattered, except for one. The sack of crackers fell from his hands as he knelt down beside the woman. When he knew that she was dead, he flung his head back and cried out. His cry was so sharp and long it was as if all the other sounds in the world suddenly died and there was only this one long cry.

Mr. Hart and Reuben had come up by this time and

taken the rifle away from Mr. Hickman, having to fight him to the ground for it. Meanwhile, as we all stood watching, the Indian leaning over the dead woman suddenly lifted something up out of the grass, and we were all amazed to see that he was holding a baby! It was so tiny, and had been wrapped so tightly in a sling on the woman's back, that I hadn't even taken notice of it before.

When Mr. Hart and Mr. Morrison tried to approach the Indian, he turned with the baby and ran out of sight. Frank, Hiram, and I waited by the wagons, looking down at the dead Indian woman. She was wearing a white bark dress and moccasins. A leather sling hung empty from her shoulders.

We heard that this young Sioux family had been peacefully trading for hardtack and corn from the party up ahead. Poor Frank couldn't take his eyes off the dead woman, until Mrs. Morrison and some of the others finally covered her with a blanket.

I'd rather have no pa than one who could do such a thing as what Mr. Hickman has done today. "Cold-blooded murder" is what Mr. Morrison called it. Mr. Hickman denied it, saying he was defending our train and that the Indian was preparing to fight. I don't think anyone believed him. But there was no way to prove it. And the strange thing is, even after seeing what he'd done, Mr. Hickman showed no sign of remorse.

"It was just an Injun, just a squaw," he kept muttering. Mr. Morrison was shaking with anger. He believes that all people are God's children. Reuben said that Mr. Hickman should be made to "stretch the rope" for what he done. And Mr. Hart was worried. He ordered a meeting of all the men. He said that we had to prepare ourselves in case the Indians decided to take revenge.

Tonight Mr. Morrison and I are on guard duty. Most of the train is sleeping under their wagons. I have my rifle loaded, and it's here by the fire with me as I write you. I was wondering how I'd find the courage to keep steady if we came under attack, and then I thought about you. You're my only kin, Levi. With Ma and Pa gone, we've nothing left in this world but each other. So I will do what I must to keep alive for you and for us.

It is good to be around someone like Mr. Morrison. He's not a big man, but he's strong in his beliefs and conducts himself in such a manner as to warrant respect. I hope to be like him when I'm grown. I didn't tell him how uneasy I was feeling, but I suspect Mr. Morrison knew, for as we sat together by the fire he told me how he had been afraid at times when he was growing up. Somehow it helped to hear how toads used to give him a fright when he was a small boy.

I can't help thinking about that Indian woman. Hiram figures she might have been an Indian princess, and when we asked Reuben he said we'd better pray she wasn't. She did look as if she could have been a princess, with long black hair and necklaces of beads and feathers around her neck. She seemed very young. I wonder what her life must have been like and how her baby is doing without her. The night is full of critters calling to one another in the darkness, and yet I keep hearing again and again in my mind that long, painful cry.

Your brother, Austin

Dear Levi,

There were no signs of Indians last night, but everyone is jumpy as we prepare to start out today. We are within twenty miles of Fort Laramie, and this is some comfort. The grass here is much shorter and is called buffalo grass. There is little timber to be found. It is not a pretty place. At midday Hiram and I went over to visit with Reuben. (Frank had to help his pa with a broken wheel.) Reuben gave us a drink of cider, and we sat in his wagon to get out of the sun.

We talked a lot about Mr. Hickman and what a bad thing he did. Reuben says that a person who never sees any good in others is very likely not to have many good qualities himself. I was listening to Reuben, but I couldn't help feeling curious about Old Bill. The tabby was right where it had been, on a barrel, sitting perfectly still. I finally got up the nerve and went over to it and touched its fur. It didn't budge or flicker an eyelash, and that's when I noticed that its eyes never closed the way a normal cat's do. I touched it again, and nothing.

"Reuben, I think there's something wrong with Old

Bill here," I said. "He's got some kind of malady." Reuben just laughed.

"Well, I suppose so," he said. "If you call being dead a malady."

Hiram's eyes got as big as saucers. "You mean to say he's stuffed?" he asked.

"One could phrase it so," Reuben replied. "I myself prefer to say preserved." We watched as Reuben went over and ran his hand lovingly down Old Bill's back. "Best friend I ever had," he whispered. "Traveled everywhere with me. I couldn't imagine traveling without him, and when he died I knew no other cat would ever take his place. See, Old Bill and me are orphans, and we've no family to speak of, not even a distant relative. So I found this fella outside of New Orleans who was practiced in the arts of preservation, and now Old Bill can always travel at my side."

When Reuben went to check on his kettle of soup, Hiram tried lifting Old Bill up.

"Why, he weighs more than a sack of flour," Hiram whispered. We took turns lifting him up and reckoned that he was stuffed with rocks.

When I told the Morrisons about Reuben's cat later

at supper, Mrs. Morrison made a face, but Charlotte and Lucy were eager for me to take them to Reuben's wagon for a look. Mrs. Morrison thinks it very strange to stuff a cat. I told her I supposed I understood, being an orphan myself like Reuben, that a person could love a cat if that was all they had in the way of family.

That's when Mr. Morrison got this funny expression on his face and gave Mrs. Morrison a long look. She looked back and nodded. I didn't know what to make of it until Mr. Morrison cleared his throat and proceeded to tell me how much like a son I had become to him. He asked me if I would like to settle down with him and Mrs. Morrison and the girls once we reached Oregon. He said he would help me settle Pa's claim and advise me on what I should do about it. I told him I'd like that, but I couldn't leave you behind, and do you know what he replied?

He said, "Austin, if that brother of yours is half the boy you are, we'd be glad to have him join our family, too." Charlotte and Lucy started in clapping their hands and hugging me, and they even got Mattie to clap her hands, which set us all to laughing.

Mr. Morrison and I stayed up late talking about his

plans for farming. We're going to put in a big orchard, with lots of apples and plums. Charlotte overheard us and called from the wagon, telling us to plant some peach trees for her. I told Mr. Morrison how you loved pears, so we'll have to plant pear trees, too. Mr. Morrison knows a lot about farming. He says that the best-laying hens are brown leghorns. I told him how Pa always swore by the black Spanish breeds and Mr. Morrison laughed. He says we'll have plenty of room in Oregon for all kinds of chickens, and we can have a contest to see which breed lays the most.

"You sure do have a lot of plans, Mr. Morrison," I said. He smiled and said, "That's the beauty of this land. It's ripe for plans and dreaming of all kinds."

"But what if your dreams don't come true?" I asked. "What if all your plans don't work out?"

"There's always going to be storms that you have to get through," Mr. Morrison said, shaking his head. "No doubt about it. So you grit your teeth to get through that spell of bad weather. The trick is to fix your eye on the rainbow that comes after the storm. Now, there are some folks who spend all their time planning and scheming to keep out of the rain. That's one way to stay dry, but it's no way to live, if you ask me."

The Morrisons are fine people, Levi, and we'd be part of a real family. I'm thinking about that rainbow, and in my mind I can see it stretching clear across this prairie and on over to Oregon!

Your brother, Austin

June 5, 1851

Dear Levi,

There is still no sign of Indians, though we're on the watch. The Yardlys' baby daughter fell from the wagon yesterday and was crushed to death under the wagon's wheel. It was a horrible sight and has shaken us all. There was no good timber to be found, so Mr. Yardly made a coffin out of a wooden box containing the family's silver and good dishes. Mrs. Yardly went from wagon to wagon giving away a dish here and a piece of silver there. Mrs. Morrison said the poor woman is sick with grief for the little one, who was her only daughter. Mrs. Yardly made the men dig a deep grave, for she feared the wolves would find her child.

Mr. Hart has warned us boys not to wander too far from camp, so Hiram, Frank, and I have been spending most of our time visiting with Reuben. We did do a little hunting, staying close to the wagons, and Frank shot a turkey. He was so happy, till he got up close and inspected the legs, which were rough with scales, and the claws had grown long, with thick calluses on the feet. It would most surely be tough, as it had lived a long life. But Frank said his ma would be glad for the carcass for soup, and we gave some of the feathers to Reuben. Frank's pa seems meaner than ever, hollering at Frank when we got back to camp for "wasting shot on a tough old bird." It seems nothing Frank does pleases him.

Mr. Morrison has been teaching me how to mend wheels. He's very patient as a teacher and doesn't get mad when I make a mistake, the way Mr. Hickman does with Frank.

Your brother, Austin

Dear Levi,

It's been two days since last I wrote, and so much has happened I don't know where to begin. I suppose I should start with the worst. Frank has gone. He's run away. I think he's hoping to hide out and then go west with the train behind us. Just the other day he was telling me how lucky I was to have a family as nice as the Morrisons take me in. I never thought then that he'd be looking for another family himself! It seems his pa gave him another whipping last night.

When I woke up this morning I found his snakeskin in my pack, and Hiram found his fossil rock outside his wagon. I had a sick feeling in my stomach when I saw that skin, 'cause I knew how much it meant to Frank, and I knew how bad he must have felt having to run away in these desolate parts.

Hiram and I spent a good part of the morning looking for him and calling his name, but if he heard us, he never answered. It was decided at supper that a group of men would go out searching at first light tomorrow, but Mr. Hart warned that we couldn't afford to stop longer than a few hours, as our supplies are running low.

Mr. Morrison has volunteered to go along with Hiram's pa and a few others. Mr. Hickman looks as miserable as ever, and it's hard to tell if he misses Frank or not. Hiram and I surely do.

Sometimes I lie awake a long time listening to the coyotes howling, and I think about Oregon and wonder if the land's really as beautiful as Pa said in his letters. There's been so many graves along this trail that I'm grateful he made it out to Oregon. I'd hate to think of him left out here with nothing but dust and the wolves. I hope Frank has found a good hiding place.

Your Brother, Austin

June 10, 1851

Dear Levi,

A most terrible thing has happened. About an hour after Mr. Morrison and the others went out searching for Frank, who should come limping into camp but Frank himself! It seems he was only a few yards away all the while, hiding in some tall grass. His foot never healed proper, and when the pain started up again, he decided to come back. We were all much relieved, and Mr. Hart sent a man out to call in the search party.

Hiram and I were playing with Charlotte and Lucy when we heard the shots. It wasn't long before Mr. Hickman and the others came riding back into camp. Mr. Morrison was not with them. Then Hiram's pa walked up to Mrs. Morrison and bowed his head. When he looked up and I saw his eyes, I knew what he was going to say.

"I'm sorry, Mrs. Morrison, but Tom's dead," he said. "He's been shot by Indians. We couldn't get to him. We barely got out with our lives."

I couldn't watch anymore, because my eyes were filling up with tears. Then Hiram came up and stood beside me, but it was as if he were a hundred miles away. It was the strangest feeling, as if I were all alone and no one could reach me. It was just the way I felt when Pa died.

Mr. Hart has called for everyone to arm themselves, and he's sent a messenger to the fort. Mrs. Morrison is beside herself with grief, and I've had to look after the girls, who are as heartsick as their mother. I cannot understand how someone as good and kind as Mr. Morrison was killed because of Mr. Hickman's wrongdoing. Why didn't they kill Mr. Hickman? I can't help feeling that he was the one who should have died, for he was the one that fired the gun and murdered that Indian woman, and he was the one that drove his own son away.

Mr. Hickman started right in again on Frank for having run away, and he tried to say that Mr. Morrison's death was on account of Frank, but Mr. Hart stepped in and said that the Indians most likely hadn't forgotten about their squaw and would have attacked anyway for revenge. But likely as that may be, Frank's sure to get the switch.

Poor Mr. Morrison was the kindest, most gentle man

I ever met, and it seems such a bitter mistake that he should have to die. I'm trying hard to school in my sadness, but it's not easy. Mr. Morrison was so like a pa to me. He taught me to swim and to mend an axle, and he was planning on showing me how to farm. It's hard now to think of Oregon without him. All those plans he had for us, for the orchard, and the chickens.

As I tucked Charlotte into her bed tonight she asked me if her pa could hear her in heaven. I told her I supposed he could, and she said she was glad because now she would talk to him every night so he wouldn't be lonely. As I write you I can hear Mrs. Morrison's low sobs and little Charlotte whispering softly about peach trees, and I feel as if all the sadness in the world has settled in this wagon tonight.

Your grieved brother, Austin

Dear Levi,

The militia arrived yesterday, and they were a sight. They seemed very courageous in their fine blue uniforms, and the officers had sabers that glistened in the sunlight. The general rode right into our camp, and he and Mr. Hart had a long talk. Hiram and I fetched water for his horse. Hiram even cut a piece of the horse's tail for a keepsake. He said he never got so close to a horse belonging to a general in the U.S. Army!

There are hundreds of soldiers on horseback. Their uniforms seem very fine. Everyone feels much relieved with them here, especially since we've learned that there is a large Sioux village close by. The only one not happy about the situation is Reuben. He says the Indians have taken one of ours for one of theirs, and the way they see it, justice has been served. But the army doesn't see it that way. They don't count an Indian's life worth as much as a white man's. Reuben says they can be more savage than the Indians.

Mrs. Morrison asked me if I thought I could stay on with her and help her get to Oregon, now that Mr.

Morrison is gone. Mr. Buckner, Hiram's pa, has offered to help when he can, and Mr. Yardly came by and checked all our wheels for us. I know it will be a struggle once we start moving again, but I cannot let Mrs. Morrison and the girls down. I am the man of the wagon now.

After supper Mrs. Morrison took me aside and handed me a bundle tied in string.

"These are all Tom's maps," she whispered. "I know that he would have wanted you to have them."

I didn't open them up, but kept them tied in the string. Later that night I took them to bed with me.

Your brother, Austin

Dear Levi,

It has been two days, and we've just received word
from the militia that we can continue on. There will be
no threat of Indian attack, as the army has gone into
the Sioux village and killed them all. We could hear the
gunfire from here. The estimate was four hundred Indians
dead and two soldiers killed. Some people in camp are
calling it a victory. I don't see it that way and neither
does Reuben.

"A victory is when something has been won," he
said. "What has been won here? Four hundred lives
have been taken, and because they are not white-skinned
people, because they have different dress and ways, we
celebrate their deaths. But had they been white, what
would we have called it then? Victory? No. Slaughter."

As I stood there with Reuben in his button-covered
coat, I suddenly realized how differently he looks at
things. Most people stick to their own kind, but maybe
because Reuben is alone in the world he feels no special
kinship to any one kind of people. He feels a kinship to
all people.

I wonder that so many on our train feel cause to celebrate. I think about that Indian baby now, and I feel ashamed.

Your brother, Austin

Dear Levi,

It must be about a hundred degrees in the shade, if there was any shade, and I can guarantee you there is not! We crossed Devil's Crater today, the most desolate and rough piece of ground that was ever made. There is not a drop of water or a spear of grass—nothing but cracked, dry prairie, rock, and dust. Without Mr. Morrison it is very hard on me, as I do most of the driving, taking turns on and off with Mrs. Morrison. The sand is ankle deep, and it is very slow going.

Hiram was walking beside me yesterday when suddenly we heard a loud rattling sound. I looked down to see the biggest rattlesnake I had ever laid eyes on. (It was much bigger than the one we saw last spring by Cuttler's Creek.) And it was inches from Hiram's foot! We both knew that if either of us moved the snake would attack, so we stood stock-still, hoping someone would see us. It was so close that we were afraid to call out! Reuben had made up a supper for us, since Mrs. Morrison was feeling poorly, and as he walked toward us the snake stretched and rattled some more. It didn't

take Reuben more than a second to reach for his revolver, and with one shot that snake was laid down.

We counted thirteen rattles. When we opened the
snake up, we found two prairie dog puppies and an owl
egg in its stomach. Hiram and I couldn't decide on who
should get the skin. He said he should since it was his
foot that was closest. We finally decided to take turns
keeping it, and he's got it hanging off his belt hook right
now. Frank came by and told me he heard Hiram brag-
ging to the Yardly boys that he wrestled the snake to
the ground with his bare hands before Reuben finally
shot it. I'm surprised he gave Reuben any credit at all!

Mrs. Morrison is looking very worn out, as the baby
she's been expecting is due any time now. If the baby
is a boy, she plans to name him Thomas Austin. I felt
sad and happy on hearing this.

Your brother, Austin

Dear Levi,

We passed Independence Rock this morning, and there looked to be a million names carved on it. At noon we came to Devils Gate. I have never seen such a wonder in my life. The Sweetwater River passes through a gap, or gate, as it's called, of the Rocky Mountains. It passes right through the mountain of solid rock about two rods wide. The rocks are more than two hundred feet high, and even the tallest man seems very small standing next to them.

We crossed Sweetwater River on a bridge (which I was most grateful for). Mrs. Morrison had to pay three dollars. The stock had to be swum across, but the current was so swift, the horses kept turning back. There were Snake Indians on the shore who were offering to swim the animals across in trade for corn, coffee, or whiskey. These were the first Indians we've come upon since Fort Laramie, and everyone was nervous. Reuben spoke to them and told us that they were friendly. He was the first to trade to have his mule swum across. After that, most of the rest of us followed, excepting

Mr. Hickman, who almost drowned when his oxen turned midstream.

The water here is alkali and poison. One of Mr. Belshaw's horses died after drinking some. I had a hard time keeping our stock away from it. There are many copperheads here.

Your brother, Austin

Dear Levi,

We saw our first buffalo today! I had stopped to fix a harness when I heard what I thought to be a thunderstorm. I looked to the west and saw a great moving black cloud in the distance. As it came closer I saw that it was indeed a herd of buffalo, their noses to the ground and their tails flying midair. Something had stirred them, for they were stampeding, and it was easy to tell that anything in their path was sure to be mowed down.

A couple of Mr. Hart's men took off on horses and brought two of the beasts down. Reuben was not very pleased. He told me that the buffalo is a walking storehouse, what with the meat from the hump and tongue and marrowbone. Then there's the skin and fur for covering and the chips for fuel. He said that since we had neither the proper utensils to make use of the massive beasts, nor the time to spare for such preparations, it was sinful to let so much go to waste.

But as he prepared what meat he could (the humps and tongues), Reuben said it should prove especially tender and flavorful because it came from cows, not bulls. He said the men were lucky to bring down a buffalo cow, since they can outrun the bulls. After the stampede we collected buffalo chips and used them to make a fire. Reuben stripped the hind legs of flesh and buried them in the coals of the chips. In an hour baked marrow was served. It was the most delicious thing I've tasted yet on this trip.

Reuben and some of the women hung strips of meat outside the wagons to cure for jerky. Mrs. Morrison was worried about wolves smelling the meat and coming around at night, so she wouldn't have any. She seems to be more anxious and fearful with each passing day. I'm teaching Charlotte to milk the cows, and she has even helped me to yoke the cattle.

Your brother, Austin

Dear Levi,

Reuben says that we should reach the shores of the Columbia in little more than four weeks' time. Traveled twenty-three miles to the Snake River today, through Pawnee country. We did not see any Pawnee, and Reuben says that's a good thing. He says that Indians are no different from white men in that there are good and bad in both races. He said many of the Pawnee are at war with the Sioux, who are peaceful and look to be left alone. Reuben says that if the U.S. Army had only known more about the situation in Nebraska and how peaceful the Sioux are, they could have spared that village.

We crossed Swamp Creek this morning and Goose Creek this afternoon. The banks along Goose Creek go almost straight up and then straight down. A number of things pitched out of the wagons, including Lucy! She was shaken up, but not hurt bad.

This prairie stretches out as far as my eye can see, with nothing growing on it but a brown grass and a greenish gray sagebrush. When we first came upon it, the sage was pleasant to smell, but after walking through miles and miles of the stuff, I soon grew weary of its scent. When the wind blows, the grass rolls back and forth like so many waves of water. Reuben says it reminds him of the sea. Never having seen an ocean, I couldn't rightly say, though looking at all that swaying grass gave Mrs. Morrison a bout of dizziness. Reuben offered a tonic of herbs he said was especially helpful for seasickness!

There is no good water to be found except in some mud puddles by the side of the road or the green slimy water standing at the bottom of ravines. Frank and I were so thirsty this afternoon that we shut our eyes and took a drink from a mud puddle. When I think of all the puddles I used to jump in and over back home, I can hardly believe that I'm now drinking from them!

Your thirsty brother, Austin

Dear Levi,

We have not come very far in the last few days, as the road is rocky and we seem to spend all our time pushing, pulling, and dragging our wagons along. To dampen our spirits even further, we must pass by the evidence of those who have failed before us, for the road is littered with broken wheels, axles, and whole wagons that have been left behind. Sometimes I am astonished that we have come this far at all.

I often daydream of Pennsylvania and its soft, rolling hills, good roads, and sturdy houses. I've been thinking a lot about houses of late, and how much I'd like to sleep in one, on a good bed with clean sheets and a real feather pillow. All this talk of beds has got me shutting my eyes, so I will say good night.

Your brother, Austin

July 20, 1851

Dear Levi,

We are camped in a strange place full of bubbling springs. We learned that the springs are called Soda Springs, or Steamboat Springs, and I can certainly see why. The hot water bubbles right up out of the ground. Hiram's mother made a cup of tea by just scooping up some water and pouring it over the tea leaves. It is great fun to throw sticks and stones into these jets and watch them rise almost three feet high! Near one spring there is an air hole that makes the sound of a steamboat, but not loud. When I tried some of the water it was hot and I had to spit it out. It was so unpleasant, like soda water without any syrup, only a metal taste.

The women are determined that we all have a bath, but it was hard to find a spring with water cool enough to bathe in. We finally did, but it was still very hot.

Your brother, Austin

Dear Levi,

We are traveling along the Snake River. Hiram caught a horned toad today, and it is truly amazing. The Yardly boys offered to trade their marbles for it and Toby Nelligan offered his hoop, but Hiram says he won't take any such trifles. When he brought it to show Reuben and me, Reuben warned him that toads cause warts and Hiram instantly let go of his hold on the thing. We had a hard time finding him after that, for he had hopped into Reuben's wagon. After looking all over, where do you suppose that toad got to? We found him sitting as still as a statue on Old Bill's back! If the two of them didn't make a sight. Hiram went to lay a hand on him, and he jumped right out of the wagon and vanished before we could jump out ourselves.

The mosquitoes woke us this morning, and we yoked up at first light to drive on and be rid of them. I feel sorriest for the animals, for they can do little to shake them off. Our ox Big Abe is covered with bites that have swelled to the size of a fist. Reuben has rubbed him down with one of his concoctions, and it seems to

75

help. I guess I was looking as sorry as Abe, what with all my bites, so Reuben fixed up a bad-smelling concoction of roots and herbs for me as well. When I admired a dried gourd he had hanging inside his wagon, he untied it and gave it to me. It is long and twisty, and when you shake it, it sounds like a rattler. It is just curled enough that I can slip it through my belt hook. Reuben says that you can keep away many harmful insects with shaking it, as they don't take to the sound.

Mrs. Morrison looks very sad to me. I know she is concerned about the new baby, and I hope we reach a settlement soon. For myself, I will be glad to sleep under a solid roof again, drink some good clean cold water, and see some shady green trees.

I think about you and wonder how you're getting on and if you've sprouted up much since I left. You would hardly recognize me, as I'm taller by an inch at least and my skin is darker than a walnut's, though it's hard to tell through the layers of dust that have piled up on me!

Your brother, Austin

Dear Levi,

We have reached Fort Boise, and it is not what I expected. There were three new buildings filled with soldiers, Hudson's Bay Company officials, some Frenchmen, and some Indians. It didn't look much like a fort at all, but one of the soldiers explained that it would be someday. He walked about with Reuben and me, showing us where the stockade was underway and where the other buildings would eventually go. He said it will be a "stronghold to reckon with one day." I would have liked to stay longer, but everyone is anxious to move on, seeing how we are so close to reaching the shore of the Columbia.

We are losing cattle every day. The road is dry and dusty, and there seems to be no end to the dead horses, oxen, mules, and cows that line the road. Along with these are yokes, chains, buggies, and even wagons that have been left. Everyone feels uneasy having to walk by such sights. One of our calves took sick and died yesterday morning, and a good milk cow died this afternoon. Mr. Hart said it was due to bad water or weeds.

The Buckners' ox Old Dave just dropped dead in the yoke. The smell from the dead cattle is very bad, and we've decided to push on farther to get away from it. Reuben says the wolves will be feasting tonight.

The other evening we saw a herd of about fifty of them, and they began howling and didn't let up till sunrise. Added to this was the hooting of owls. You never heard such a racket! Mrs. Morrison is very frightened to hear the wolves, and I have to admit it is a fearsome sound.

Reuben knows a lot about wolves and their ways. He says there are many different kinds of them on the prairie. There is the common gray prairie wolf, the black wolf, and another, a large, long-legged wolf. This long-legged one is called a buffalo ranger, as it stalks the buffalo, often bringing down a calf. These wolves are most ferocious and will attack a man if hungry.

After supper last night, Reuben got out his Jew's harp and Mr. Buckner took out his fiddle. Some folks got up to dance, and Charlotte pulled on my arm until I thought it would fall off. So I got up to dance with her but didn't know the steps. Mrs. Yardly offered to give us a lesson, and by the last tune we were almost getting it right. Frank and Hiram had a good laugh at my expense, but it was worth it to see Mrs. Morrison smiling again. I wonder what the wolves thought about our carrying on.

Hope you are well,
Your brother, Austin

Dear Levi,

It is hard to believe how many miles we've come! And yet we still have a ways to go before we reach the Columbia River.

Hiram, Frank, and I were following a trail not far from the road, collecting lava stones, when we spotted a grizzly! It must have been eight hundred pounds or more and at least eight feet tall standing. Its paws were as big as both my hands together. Luckily we were far enough away, and downwind, so it did not pick up our scent. Frank's pa told us never to shoot at a grizzly alone, because when fired at they start immediately for the place where the gun cracked, yet one ball rightly put in will kill them as easily as a buffalo.

Frank had his rifle, I had my bowie knife, and all Hiram had was his slingshot, but Frank's hands were trembling so bad we didn't think to risk it. We just stayed put and watched as the great bear turned and wandered off over a hill. We would certainly have been heroes if we had returned to camp with such a prize as a grizzly, but I was glad just to be able to see it. I think it would have been a sad deed to put down such a great beast.

"He looked as if he was going to attack us, wouldn't you say?" Hiram said on the way back to camp. "And he was at least ten, maybe twelve, feet tall, wouldn't you say?" By the time we reached the wagons, Hiram had so embroidered on the truth that Frank and I breathed a sigh of relief.

Walking across this country offers a boy more excitement than he could ever find at home. The truth is that every now and then I long for those quiet times when you and I sat out on Miss Amelia's back porch with a bowl of her vanilla-bean ice cream and the smell of peach pie drifting out of her kitchen. Pennsylvania sure seems a long way away.

Your brother, Austin

Dear Levi,

We've come some twenty miles since last I wrote you. The country here is rough and the road very rocky, but we've found some good grass for grazing the cattle, who are looking thin and worn out. There is also good water here from the mountain streams. There are steep mountains with snow on the peaks. The nights are bitter cold, and yet by noon time the sun is sizzling hot. We had to stop yesterday, for the Mendlesons' wagon broke down, with the tongue needing repairs, and the Yardlys' axle was ready to give out. While we waited, Frank and I climbed up a ledge and got a bucket of snow water to drink. When Hiram came looking for us, we surprised him with an attack of snowballs!

Coming down, I picked a handful of blue and yellow flowers for Mrs. Morrison, as I know blue is her favorite color. Frank found the horns of a mountain goat and was glad to have them.

When we got back to camp, Reuben made a pot of sage hen soup and offered some to us, as Mrs. Morrison was feeling poorly again. He also brought us some broiled prairie dog, which Mrs. Morrison refused to eat. I tasted a bit, and it seemed very much like turkey to me, though I could not persuade Mrs. Morrison to try any. Last night the rocks lit up with the glow of our fires, and you could smell the pine trees very strongly. As hard as this road is to travel, it is sometimes a beautiful place.

Your brother, Austin

Dear Levi,

It grieves me to have to write you that Mrs. Morrison
has died. She took to her bed inside the wagon just two
days ago. Mrs. Yardly attended her, as did Mrs. Taylor,
but they could not save her or the new baby boy that
was born. We had been traveling high over a mountain,
and the road was especially rocky and difficult. I can't
help but think the two would have lived had we made
it to the settlement. It is pitiful to hear Lucy and
Charlotte's cries for their mother, and even Mattie seems
inconsolable. As I watched them wrap Mrs. Morrison
and the new baby together in a quilt to be buried, I felt
as if a cold wind was blowing through my heart. Mr.
Buckner made a headstone from a wagon wheel found
along the road.

Later Mr. Yardly and a group of others came by to
talk to me. It was decided that the wagon would be
taken apart, since there was no use hauling it any farther. I know Mrs. Morrison would have wanted the
girls to remain together, but there is no one here who
can afford to take on three extra children. Mrs. Buckner

has offered to take in Charlotte and Lucy, and Mrs. Yardly, who lost her own little girl, will take Mattie. They will divide up the cattle. Most of Mrs. Morrison's things will have to be left behind. That left only me to decide about.

I suppose I must go back to my first plan and look for work in the lumber camp once we reach the Columbia River. But we still have a way to go, and I needed to travel with someone. Everyone got real quiet, and then Mr. Hickman stepped up and said he supposed he could use an extra hand. Frank's eyes grew bigger than silver dollars at this suggestion, and I felt my stomach sink at the thought of having to live under that cruel man's eye, but I didn't see any other way until Reuben came walking around the wagon.

"Oh, no, you don't," he said. "I've been looking for a good pot scrubber for a long while, and besides, Austin here and I are already friends. What do you say to coming along with me and Old Bill, boy?"

I looked down at the moon-faced button on my coat, and I felt myself starting to grin. So it's all settled. I'm to travel the rest of the way with Old Bill and Reuben McAlister Rice!

Reuben and I sat for a long while and talked about getting on in the world. Reuben says you can never know what will befall you, and it wasn't hard for me to agree. He says the most important thing he's learned is that you must always be prepared to bend with whichever way the breeze is blowing, or like a brittle tree, you'll snap. I said I felt that if I did much more bending I'd have a hard time ever straightening up again.

I couldn't get to sleep for thinking about Mrs. Morrison and her rocking chair and how I couldn't bear to just leave it on the side of the road. So the next morning Frank and I got up early and carried it to a little grove where there were some blue flowers growing, and we set it there. Later on as the wagons started to roll and we began heading out, we passed the wooden marker with EMILY MORRISON AND HER BABY SON THOMAS AUSTIN MORRISON carved on it. I turned my face away, feeling too sad for words, and it was then that I spied her chair in the distance, where Frank and I had placed it. It was the saddest sight I ever saw, for the wind had picked up, and that empty chair had begun to rock all by itself in that field of pretty blue flowers.

Your brother, Austin

Dear Levi,

We are waiting our turn to cross the Snake River, after which we'll follow the trail through the Blue Mountains. There is one small ferryboat that will take the wagons across. It is owned by the Hudson's Bay Company. This is a large river, and it is very hard getting the stock over. There are Indians who do nothing but swim the river from morning till night. Reuben thinks they are of the Rogue River tribe. After all the stock lost, everyone is grateful to pay the Indians to do this. Even Mr. Hickman has paid to have his cattle crossed.

Reuben has only one ox to care for, and two mules, so I reckon I'll have an easier time, though he wasn't fooling about that pot scrubbing! He cooks for eight men, and that makes for a mess of pots as well as plates. But working with Reuben is truly fun, for he's always whistling and working alongside me, telling funny stories and making me laugh.

Hiram, being a small boy, has been having some problems with bigger boys picking on him. There are two bullies who seem intent on tormenting him. These are the Judson brothers, Zeb and Stuart. They are built like mountains, with great big bodies and very little brains, and they've taken to shoving Hiram and knocking him down. They haven't the courage to harm him when Frank or I are about. I feel sorry for Hiram, as he must always be on the lookout, and he carries his slingshot wherever he goes now. The three of us have decided to stay together as much as we can.

Yesterday we found a beaver's dam as we neared the river. It was made from the willows that line the banks. The branches were cut so clean and smooth you'd swear it had to be the work of a hatchet. The whole construction was layered with sticks neatly laid. Above this they had thrown moss and leaves, which, catching the sand, had completely stopped the water and raised it three feet. The dam was some forty feet long. Reuben told me that the Indians believe the beaver has a great soul, and on seeing such work as this dam, I believe it.

After having a good look, we decided to hide in some brush so as to catch sight of the beavers. We spent a long while waiting, and every now and then I'd give the gourd Reuben gave me a shake to keep away the buffalo gnats that were attacking us. To pass the time, Hiram showed us his crooked toe, Frank showed his two warts, and I showed off the long scar I got from slipping on that rock last year. When we heard a splash, we all looked up to see a beaver going about his work. This was the first beaver I had ever laid eyes on, and he looked very much like a muskrat to me, except that he was larger, with a big broad tail that was flat, hard, and scaly like a fish. His teeth were like a squirrel's, only much larger. He seemed very strong indeed.

We were having great fun watching him build his dam when suddenly we saw a rock come flying straight for him. The beaver was quick to dive underwater, and when we looked to see where the rock had come from, who should come out of the brush but Zeb Judson and his brother, Stuart. The bullies swaggered over to the beavers' dam and proceeded to tear into it.

We were outraged, as we had seen how hard our beaver had worked (and by now we did think of him as "our beaver"). Hiram raised his slingshot and muttered something about "protecting the dam." He seemed willing to risk all for the sake of the beavers until I persuaded him to put down his slingshot. Then I had an idea, which I promptly whispered to my comrades.

Within minutes Frank jumped out of the brush and screamed, "Snakes! Snakes! Rattlesnakes!" Hiram jumped out, yelling, "It's a whole mess of them! Run for your lives!" I waited a few seconds for the Judson boys to look up, and then as I lay out of sight I began shaking that gourd as hard as I could.

At the sound of those seeds rattling around in the gourd, the two bullies lit out of there faster than a jack rabbit.

Back at camp we found them huffing and puffing and telling anyone who would listen about the nest of rattlers they almost stepped on. Then what does Hiram do but puff out his chest and walk right up to Zeb, the biggest, and say loudly, so everyone can hear:

"Gee, boys, you sure can run fast when you're a-scared."

The Judsons gave him a queer look back. Then Hiram turned to me and gave the gourd on my belt a shake. "Never saw anybody run so fast at the sound of a few seeds shaking," he said.

This set everyone to laughing—everyone excepting the Judsons, of course. They looked mad enough to foam at the mouth! Hiram may be small, but he's got the spunk of someone twice his size.

Later in the day Reuben asked us to hunt him up some "sweet black mice for a pie." We were lucky enough to run into a nest of them along the riverbank, and he was much pleased with our catch. I had a harder time tasting the mice pie than I did the prairie dogs, and finally could not bring myself to eat any, though Reuben claimed it was "very delicious."

Your brother, Austin

August 18, 1851

Dear Levi,

I hope you are well. I was sick with a fever for three days and so could not celebrate the fact that we have almost reached the shores of the Columbia. But I'm feeling better today. Charlotte was also sick, though Lucy and Mattie are well. I try to visit with them every day, as they have become orphans like me, and I think of them as sisters.

Frank's family had a bad accident yesterday. Their lead mule Ned, spooked by something on the side of the road, shied suddenly to the right. He turned so short that Mr. Hickman had no time to stop him, and *crack! crack! crack!*—away went the tongue of their wagon. It was nearly broken off, but fortunately in long splinters.

Frank's pa set to cussing and then drew his revolver. "This'll teach you," he snarled, and put a ball through one of Ned's thighs. The poor mule danced around in pain before finally settling down. It took near an hour to fix the wagon's tongue, since the other men on the train seemed reluctant to offer their help—even Mr.

Hickman's brother-in law, Mr. Cantrell. But everyone knew that the sooner the tongue was repaired the sooner we could all move on, so Mr. Cantrell and a number of the others finally did come forward.

Frank's face went all red, as it always does when his father draws attention to himself. We stood around watching them cut some rawhide strips to tie up the broken pieces, when Ned suddenly lets loose with both hind feet as Mr. Hickman draws near. There was a loud whoosh of air as Frank's pa was struck in the chest. He fell over backward, with his hat falling off his head. When he stood back up, I knew he was aiming to kill Ned, and I guess Ned knew it, too, 'cause as soon as Mr. Hickman came at him with his revolver again, the mule turned and with his left hind leg kicked Mr. Hickman in the side of the head. When Frank's pa fell this time, he didn't get back up.

They carried him to his wagon, and Reuben did what he could, though he thought a doctor was needed. Mr. Cantrell rode out to the train ahead, where a doctor is traveling, and in a short time the man arrived to attend to him. I told Reuben how surprised I was to see Frank looking so worried, since his pa was such a bad man.

Reuben said that folks are never just good or bad, and most times they've got some good and bad mixed up in them, though he supposed Mr. Hickman had more bad than good. He also said "Blood is thicker than water," and that as mean as Frank's pa was to him, he was the only pa Frank had.

We finally moved out today, with Mr. Hickman still taken to his bed in his wagon. He came down with a fever last night, so the doctor rode over late this afternoon and bled him, but Frank says he does not seem much improved.

Neither Hiram nor I really wanted to do it, but for Frank we knew we should, so we both decided on including Mr. Hickman in our prayers.

Your brother, Austin

Dear Levi,

Frank's pa died this morning. There was a heavy frost on the ground, and it took the men a while to dig the grave. Mrs. Hickman did not shed a tear as she watched the men making a coffin out of wagon pieces found on the road. Frank stayed near his mother and would not come near Hiram or me. Mr. Cantrell, Mrs. Hickman's brother, will help them to finish the journey, and Frank's older brother Ben will do most of the driving.

We got a late start on account of the burial and only made ten miles. There are a great many evergreen trees here, fir and pine, and it looks very much like the green of Pennsylvania.

I saw a fine hummingbird with a brilliant scarlet red head and a body of bright yellow, with the outer half of its wings being scarlet, too.

A number of Snake warriors galloped near to us but then rode off. They were wearing feathered headdresses and had handsome horses with red blankets. They seemed very fine indeed.

We passed near the Indian lodges where there was a large grove of serviceberries. Many of the ripe berries had been picked and dried, and the squaws were offering to trade a half-bushel of the fruit for a darning needle. Reuben said he had a good recipe for berry cobbler, but when he looked behind the Indians, he found that the berries had been laid to dry on the flesh side of green deerskins spread on the ground. There were flies, dirt, and dogs all gathering about, and so he decided against berry cobbler that night.

We saw a flock of wild geese at a nearby stream, and Reuben is determined to bring one back for tomorrow's dinner. I almost went with him, but then decided to work on my slingshot with Frank instead. Seeing how we've become Hiram's protectors, and he has the bad habit of shooting his mouth off to any bully that crosses his path, we thought it best to arm ourselves.

It is getting darker as I write this by the fire, and I wonder where Reuben has got to, as he usually returns before dark. Sometimes it's hard to imagine how far we've come and how far away you are, Levi. I try not to dwell on that too much, but rather on the day that we'll be together again, living on Pa's claim. I hope you haven't forgotten me too much.

Your brother, Austin

Dear Levi,

It seems every time I settle in with someone, it all goes bad. Reuben did not return to camp last night. Mr. Hart is very worried, as it is most unlike Reuben to stay out overnight. Early this morning a number of cattle were riled up, and two mules had taken off. Mr. Hart suspects a panther, as one was spotted yesterday. All I can think of is Reuben meeting up with such a beast. I know he is quick with his gun, but I wonder how quick one must be to survive a panther's attack.

There was also word this morning from the train ahead of us that a scalp had been found pinned to a tree with an arrow through it. Mr. Hart did not think this could be the work of Indians in these parts, as they are not known to take scalps. No one seems to know who took the scalp or whose head it came from.

They did not say what color the scalp was, and Hiram says that's a good sign, since Reuben's hair is so red they surely would have mentioned the color. I am not so sure. As we waited for the search party to return,

Frank suggested we pick some wild garlic behind the wagons.

"Reuben can use it when he fixes that goose he's bringing back," he said. Hiram was quick to agree, but I didn't say anything. I was thinking about the time Reuben and I talked about life and how nothing stays the same and how the wind is always fixing to change course.

As set as I was on receiving bad news, I wasn't near prepared enough for what happened next. Hiram's ma was scrubbing some things in a bucket, back of their wagon, when she lets out a holler. By the time Hiram, Frank, and I reached her, she looked as if she'd seen a ghost. She didn't say a word, just pointed to a hill close to our train. There I saw three Indians on horseback. Two were dressed in skins of some sort, but it was the third that stopped my heart, for he was wearing Reuben's button coat!

When Mr. Buckner called to them, the Indians took off. Mr. Hart said that it might prove too dangerous to send a party after them. I heard him tell Mr. Yardly that he sorely regretted having to lead the train, or he'd go after the Indians himself. Everyone is very sad, but none sadder than me, I think. Tonight I will sleep in the wagon alone, just me and Old Bill. I wish the wind would calm down for a while and stop changing its course. I'm feeling chilled to the bone.

Your brother, Austin

Dear Levi,

I am so glad to write you about the events of this morning. I had slept poorly and was up early, when I heard a ruckus coming from outside the wagon. I pulled back the flap and who should be standing with his back to me but an Indian warrior in full feathered headdress! I let out a holler so loud that I woke up most of the train. The Indian spun around with a goose in his hand, and my mouth dropped open, for I could see that this Indian had a red beard. And then I realized that it wasn't an Indian at all. It was Reuben!

By this time folks were coming out of their wagons and gathering around us. Everyone was talking and laughing and much relieved to see that Reuben was alive. When everyone calmed down and had enough of touching his headdress, Reuben started in to tell us what happened.

Just before sundown yesterday he had shot himself a good fat goose. He was heading back to camp when his mule, Chester, fell into a badger's hole. He had a hard time getting him out, as the mule's leg was twisted pretty bad. Reuben knew if he tried to force the mule back to camp on a bad leg, he'd probably lame him for good. So he wrapped the leg in some dock leaves and settled in to spend the night, hoping that by morning Chester would be improved.

After making a fire to warm himself, Reuben set about plucking his goose, when he heard some branches breaking behind him. That's when the three Cayuse Indians appeared. They had just come from some big powwow, and Reuben deduced at once that the one wearing a splendid headdress was a chief. Reuben could see that this chief was very proud and strong, but he seemed friendly enough. When the chief offered to trade his headdress for the coat, Reuben knew better than to refuse.

"It was plain they fancied my red hair almost as much as my coat, so I thought it best to give up the coat and with luck keep my scalp. I suppose that chief was under the impression that I was some great chief myself, what with having such a coat. He was most respectful in making the transaction and seemed quite satisfied as he mounted his pony. I declare, it was mighty hard to see my old coat with all its years of buttons go riding off on that

Indian's back, though I reckon he's as respectful of its worth as I could hope for."

Frank, Hiram, and I all took turns trying on the headdress, which has all kinds of feathers in many colors and a band of very fine beadwork. Later that night we enjoyed a feast of roast goose, and Reuben noted that the flavor was much improved by the fresh garlic.

As we were clearing up, I told Reuben how worried I had been. He said I worry too much and that it wasn't good for my "constitution." Then I asked him if he would get another coat, so that he could collect more buttons on his travels.

"I suppose I'm growing weary of traveling and making camp every night," Reuben replied. "I was thinking I might try settling down for a spell."

I took a deep breath before asking him if he would settle in Oregon, and he said he thought he would.

"So this new coat could be your Oregon coat," I suggested.

He smiled at that and said, "I suppose so."

That's all he would say on the subject, but it was enough to make me feel a whole lot easier about finding my way out here. At least I know I have a friend in Reuben. I can hardly believe that in two weeks' time I'll be looking out over Pa's "beautiful acres"!

Your brother, Austin

Dear Levi,

We are camped very close to the Columbia River! Last night we had a dinner of fried salmon. There are many Indians camped around us selling these fish to the trains. We crossed the Fall, or Deschutes River, as it is called here. The wagons were ferried across at two dollars a wagon, and we swam the stock. I wish you could see me in the water now! I am so accustomed to it that Hiram and I had a swim just for fun after the crossing. Charlotte has taken to following us everywhere, and we gave her a ride on our backs.

Frank's ma is clean out of money and had to sell their sorrel mare, Nell, to finish the trip. It's hard to believe that we have really reached our destination! As happy as we all are, Frank and Hiram and I suddenly realized that in a short time we would have to be parting company, for we are within two days' drive of Pa's claim. Frank and Hiram will be traveling farther along with a group of others to the far northwest just outside of Fort Vancouver.

We've decided to become blood brothers. It was

Hiram's idea. He said once we became blood brothers we could never be separated by land or sea because "we'd always be united by blood." His older brother Thomas had already done it and told him how to go about it.

So we went back of the wagons and found some thorny brush, and after pulling off a sharp thorn, we pricked our fingers. Then we took turns pressing our bloodied fingers together. We swore to be secret blood brothers until the day we died. Hiram thought it would be a good idea to leave a blood print on our foreheads, so we stuck ourselves again and did that. It didn't hurt the first time, but the second time it did.

When we returned to camp, a lot of the other boys were curious about our marked foreheads, but we told them we couldn't say anything about it, as we were sworn to secrecy. I'm only telling you 'cause you're blood already.

Then we went to talk to Reuben and decided that he should be let in on it, as he had exchanged buttons with us and all. Reuben was impressed and said that having a blood brother was "truly a noble thing." He offered us each a sip of elderberry wine to mark the occasion. We also got to look through his collection of bird feathers, and we each got to choose one. Frank chose a red-winged blackbird feather, Hiram wanted the feather from a hawk, and I decided on a fine white sea gull feather that Reuben found on the beach of the Atlantic Ocean. I'm saving it for you.

We stayed up late that night talking about our feathers and the birds they came from, and Reuben made up a great tale about a blackbird, hawk, and sea gull who became friends. It was exciting and funny, and we liked it on account of its having such a happy ending. I'm glad to have reached Pa's beautiful Oregon at last, but I will surely miss the good friends I have made along the way.

Your brother, Austin

Dear Levi,

It's been pouring rain for the last two days, and we are stuck waiting here for it to let up. Seems so much harder to wait now, after coming so far, but there's nothing else to be done. I hope you are well and wonder what games you must be playing and who you're playing with. I wish I could introduce you to Frank and Hiram before we all split up. I know you would like them as much as I do. I am not good at this infernal waiting and think I might try counting raindrops to pass the time.

Your brother, Austin

Dear Levi,

Finally the rain has let up, and so much has happened, I hardly know where to begin. We crossed the Columbia River yesterday. The Cantrells have a new baby daughter, coming just before we crossed. They named her Columbia!

Frank's mother has decided to settle up north with the Cantrells, though they are camping here for another day. Since Hiram's pa was so low on money, he traded two yoke of oxen for a half-section of land with one-half acre planted to potatoes and a small cabin and lean-to with no windows. It is close enough to town and the river to make it a good location. This is where Charlotte and Lucy will live also. I wish the Buckners could take me in with them, but they have eight children now with the girls, and there is hardly enough room for them all.

Reuben has offered to help me find out about Pa's claim, and tomorrow we will go to the lumber camp and look up Mr. Zikes. Everything seems to be happening very fast.

This land is as beautiful as Pa said. The trees are

blue-green and seem to rise up hundreds of feet into the sky. I am eager to set eyes on Pa's claim and to step on the ground that he got for us.

Your brother, Austin

Dear Levi,

I visited Pa's grave today. It was out on a hill behind the lumber camp. There was a small stone marker that had heaved with the frost and was almost falling over. On it was the inscription:

MATTHEW IVES, AGED 34
DIED OF THE FEVER FEBRUARY 22, 1851

It was hard to look at that marker and think of our pa buried beneath it. Reuben helped me to right the stone and set it back in the ground.

I am sorry to have to write you that Mr. Zikes was not the friend Pa thought him to be. At the lumber camp we learned that right after Pa died, Mr. Zikes sold Pa's claim to the lumber company and took off with the money to California. The man working in the company office said we could probably buy it back, but it would have to be at a profit. Seeing how we have no money, I supposed Pa's land would be lost to us for good.

It was hard to school in my anger, anger at Mr. Zikes

for his having stole from us the only thing Pa left in this world, and anger at Pa for having trusted such a scoundrel in the first place.

As I walked out to the porch of the main building, Reuben followed me. I told him that I wished Pa had never come out here. That he should have thought of us, and what would happen to us if he was killed. That's when Reuben shook his head and said it was no good wishing for things to change that could never be changed. He said that Pa was thinking of us, and I should never forget that. Then he went back inside for a while, and I waited on the porch, stewing over all that had gone wrong.

When he came back out, Reuben didn't say anything. He just stepped off the porch and began to untie his mule. I followed him and untied mine, and together we headed back to camp. I was feeling so poorly by now that I hardly noticed we had taken a different path, and it wasn't long before Reuben brought Chester to a halt. When I asked him why we were stopping here, he stretched out his arm and said:

"To have a look." I wasn't inclined to have a look at anything, but when I finally did look out I had to admit

that it was a beautiful sight. There was a clearing surrounded by great stands of evergreens, pine, fir, and hemlock.

"That's a mighty pretty piece of property you've got yourself," Reuben said.

"What are you talking about, Reuben?" I asked.

"Talking about your pa's claim," he replied, pointing to the lake before us. "Six hundred acres, including the lake there." And that's when he told me what he had done. He had informed the man at the lumber company that he was prepared to buy back Pa's claim!

"And this, this is it?" I gasped. Reuben smiled and nodded yes. I couldn't believe my eyes! You'd have to imagine the prettiest piece of land in the States and then imagine it a hundred times prettier—that's what our claim is like. There is a stillness to these woods that runs deep, broken only by the press of the wind through the trees. There is a small lake stretching like so much glass laced with hemlock and fir. The air is pure and fresh with the scent of green wood, and the soil is rich and black.

It is all Pa said it was, and it is ours! And the best

part is that Reuben's taking on living rights—says he and Old Bill could do with a rest from the road. He's planning to cook for the lumber camp and I'll be his assistant.

"So what do you say if we build us a cabin next spring?" he asked. "I'll do the cookin', and you do the worryin'."

I was just about speechless by this time, and it was all I could do to sputter, "I could never worry as good as you cook, Reuben, but I sure would like to try!"

"Of course, we'll need that brother of yours to help with the work. So you best write him and see about his traveling out next April," Reuben said with a grin.

All is very well,
Your brother, Austin

Dear Levi,

Said good-bye to Frank today, as he and his family headed up north. Hiram gave him back his fossil rock. Frank and I exchanged lava rocks. Then we all three shook hands and pledged to remain "brothers till our dying days." It was a sad parting, as we knew we might never see Frank again.

As for Hiram, Charlotte, and Lucy, they are to be my neighbors! For our claim is only some six miles north of their cabin. Mattie is settling with the Yardlys, who are looking for a claim nearby.

This morning, as we packed up the wagon, I asked Reuben about the money for the land. It had been on my mind, since I knew he was not a wealthy man. Reuben explained how he had come into some riches several years ago but that he had found no good use for it till now. When I asked if the money was in a bank, he snorted and said he'd never trust his nuggets to a bank. That's when he went over to Old Bill and turned him over. Then he pulled on a string, and before I knew it, he was unlacing Old Bill's stomach! And what do I find but that Old Bill's stuffed with rocks all right. He's stuffed with rocks of gold!

This afternoon we'll ride over our land and decide on where to situate the cabin. The rain has cleared out, and Reuben said we might see a rainbow later on.

"Already see one," I replied.

Your brother, Austin

Author's Note

This story was inspired by the reading of original diaries of men and women who traveled along the Overland Trail between the years 1840 and 1870. During that time over a quarter of a million people made the journey across the continental United States. It was a migration of some 2,400 miles, and as the diaries make clear, it was not a trip for the faint of heart.

Among this adventurous group of pioneers were many children. I often wondered what the journey had been like for them. In researching this question, I was impressed with the strength of spirit these young travelers displayed in facing countless hardships, as well as their ability to shoulder a fair share of responsibility for their survival.

The courage and pluck of these girls and boys, living so long ago, inspired me to want to re-create their story for the children of our own time.

A Brief Bibliography

Brown, Joseph. *The Mormon Trek West*. New York: Doubleday, 1980.

Lensink, Judy N. *A Secret to Be Buried: The Diary and Life of Emily Hawley Gillespie, 1858–1888*. Iowa City: University of Iowa Press, 1989.

Schlissel, Lillian. *Women's Diaries of the Westward Journey*. New York: Schocken Books, 1982.

Schlissel, Lillian, Byrd Gibbons, and Elizabeth Hampsten. *Far from Home: Families of the Westward Journey*. New York: Schocken Books, 1989.

Stratton, Joanna L. *Pioneer Women Voices from the Kansas Frontier*. New York: Simon and Schuster, 1981.

Elvira Woodruff is a former children's librarian and professional storyteller. She has written more than a dozen picture books and novels for children, including *The Magnificent Mummy Maker; The Wing Shop,* illustrated by Stephen Gammell; and the forthcoming *Dear Austin,* the sequel to *Dear Levi.* She lives in Martins Creek, Pennsylvania, with her two sons, Noah and Jess.

Beth Peck is the illustrator of many books for children, including *A Christmas Memory* by Truman Capote and *The Snow Goose* by Paul Gallico. Her art has been called "pure and lovely" by *New York* magazine, "radiant" by *Publishers Weekly,* and "beautifully expressive" by *The Horn Book.* A graduate of the Rhode Island School of Design, Beth Peck lives with her husband and daughter in Wisconsin.